The Naughty Lamb

by Arlene Blanchard • pictures by Tony Wells

Dial Books for Young Readers • New York

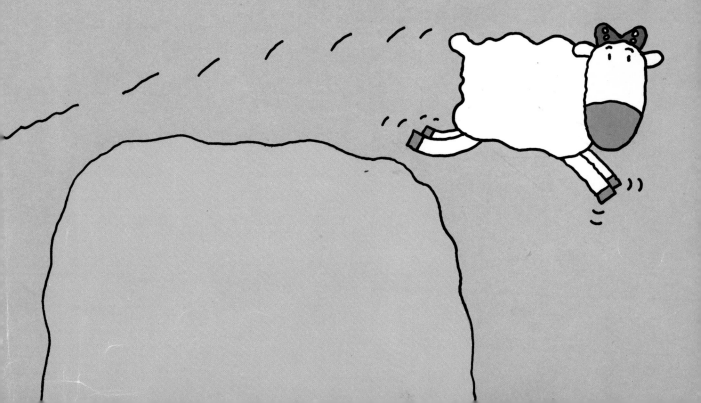

First published in the United States 1989 by
Dial Books for Young Readers
A Division of NAL Penguin Inc.
2 Park Avenue, New York, New York 10016

Published in Great Britain by Collins Picture Lions,
an imprint of the Collins Publishing Group
Text copyright © 1988 by Arlene Blanchard
Illustrations copyright © 1988 by Tony Wells
Printed in Hong Kong
First Edition
(c)
1 3 5 7 9 10 8 6 4 2

Library of Congress Cataloging in Publication Data
Blanchard, Arlene. The naughty lamb
by Arlene Blanchard; pictures by Tony Wells.
p. cm.
Summary: Ma Ma Sheep looks all over the farm for
Ba Lamb, who has decided to go exploring on her own.
ISBN 0-8037-0604-9 tr   ISBN 0-8037-0605-7 lib
[1. Sheep—Fiction. 2. Domestic animals—Fiction.
3. Farm life—Fiction.] I. Wells, Tony, ill. II. Title.
PZ7.B592Nau 1989   [E]—dc19 88-4098 CIP AC

Welcome to the farm.

This is Ba Lamb.

And this is Ma Ma Sheep.
Sometimes Ba Lamb is good and
sometimes she is a little bit naughty.

One day Ba Lamb went trotting off

just as Ma Ma Sheep was calling her for supper.

"Have you seen my Ba Lamb?"
Ma Ma Sheep asked the cows.
They blinked their big eyes.
"No," they mooed. "We don't know
where the naughty lamb is."

Do you?

Ma Ma Sheep called out to the ducks,
"Have you seen my little lamb?"
"*Quack! Quack!* She isn't with us,"
said the ducks as they splashed around
in the pond.

The chickens shook their heads at poor Ma Ma Sheep.
"Cluck! Cluck!" they said.
"What a naughty lamb to run off by herself."

Ma Ma Sheep trotted quietly past
the farm cat snoozing on the windowsill.
No point in asking her about Ba Lamb.

Ma Ma Sheep asked the mice in the barn.
"If we find Ba Lamb," they squeaked,
"we'll send her on home."

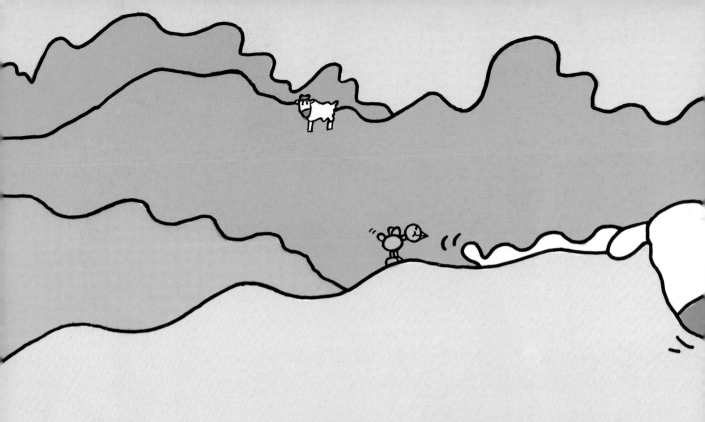

B-l-e-a-t! B-l-e-a-t!
The goats were surprised to see Ma Ma Sheep
peering over the hedge.
"Is that my Ba Lamb crying?"

"No, it's just us," they said.
"We *b-l-e-a-t* to each other all the time."

"*Neigh!*" said the horse.
"*Bray!*" said the donkey as they pranced
around the stable. "Ba did skip by.
If you hurry, you might catch up."

"*Oink! Oink!* Don't worry about your
Ba Lamb," said the pigs to Ma Ma Sheep.
"When she's hungry, she'll come and find you."

"I'm hungry now!" said the naughty lamb,
who was hiding in the bushes behind the farmhouse.

"Well then it's good that I've found you,"
said Ma Ma Sheep, "because naughty lambs
don't get dessert."

Little Ba was a good lamb all the way home.

She could be naughty another day.